NRIDEV

THE FALL OF SANPHERAN

VIVEK CHANDANSHIV

Paperback ISBN: 978-1-64953-027-1
First paperback edition: July 2020
Edited by: @maureen_zack
Book Cover by: @rebecacovers
Map by: @snikt5
Published by: Absolute Author (USA)

Absolute Author
Publishing House

https://absoluteauthor.com/

Acknowledgement

Writing a book is hard, but to pen your thoughts into a book is harder. I thank my family has always been a source of great strength to me. This book is dedicated to my loving mother, her support has made me reach where I am.

My wife who always wish me success in life and cheer me up and support me during my ups and downs.

Though I am indebted to my family and friends, the responsibility for any omissions and mistakes in the book are entirely mine.

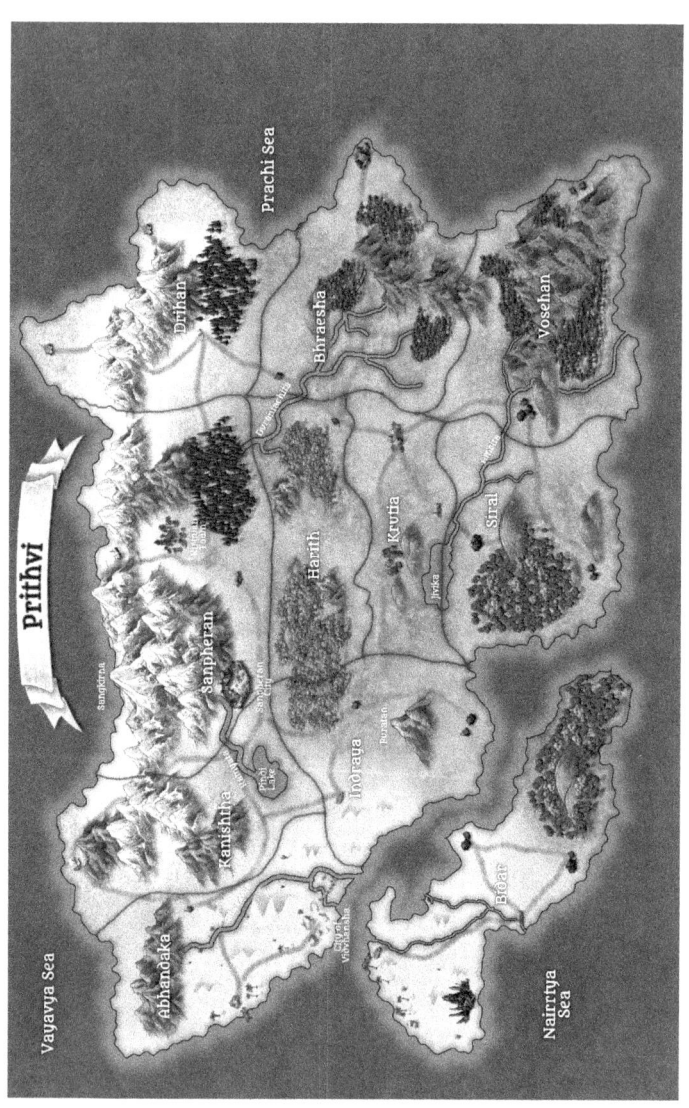

Thunderstruck and the earth shook violently as Nridev reached for the sword of the Goddess. The holy sword can be wielded only by the chosen one. Lightning lit up the dark skies. The earth trembled and split wide open under Nridev's feet. An unearthly invisible force seemed to emerge from the dark depths of the earth, gripping him, stopping him from completing the task at hand.

Our story begins in the town of Kirtiyan. A small town tucked away in the magical world of sorcery, mystical powers in the realm of Prithvi.

It is a small peaceful town far away from the bustling city of Sanpheran, the Capital of the Kingdom. The town itself is known for the School of Sword Fighting style of Ranavanya, Devavant School of Magic, and Adrishyanati School of Archery. People from other towns and cities used to come here to learn from these schools.

There are many clans in the world of Prithvi. Still, as the name of the schools suggests, Ranavanya, Devavant, and Adrishyanti Clans are the three major warrior clans of Kirtiyan, which were named after the founders of the clans, who were believed to be blessed by goddess Kirti herself. Ranavanya Clan has warriors and knights. Devavant clan has magicians and sages, and Adrishyanti clan is of Archers. They have their unique fighting styles and forms.

The towns and the cities are flush with traders from different parts of the Kingdom, hawking their wares. Markets are alive with the cries of peddlers and the laughter of jostling men women and children. Apart from the towns and cities, the rest of the realm is blessed with an abundance of natural forests and wildlife. However, what lies ahead?

Evil lurks beyond the ramparts of this Kingdom, preying on the unsuspecting travelers. Unimaginable monsters and wild animals prowl the limits of the Kingdom entrapping and slaughtering any unwary pilgrim, wayfarer, gypsy that happens to cross its way. All traders and merchant caravans are escorted by the martial forces of the Kingdom. Kirtiyan is situated in the northernmost part of Prithvi in the Kingdom of Sanpheran. There are several other kingdoms in

Prithvi, all of which live in peace and tranquility with each other.

The town of Kirtiyan is also named after the Goddess Kirti, who once saved the world from the evil which nearly destroyed Prithvi a long ago. The worshippers of the Goddess and the devotees' worship her in the Temple of Goddess Kirti, which was situated in the middle of the town.

Three friends Nridev, Nitya, and Anika were, as usual, getting ready for the day.

Nridev is a young, energetic amateur Knight, who is always ready to help others. But his luck is always on the downside. In the town, he is not that popular or loved. But always strived to get attention doing odd jobs of bounty hunting monsters and somewhat tries to make a living. His parents were long gone, and he was trying to make a living in this harsh world all by himself.

Nitya is a magician who always experiments with the Magic. He is well-known as a sloppy magician who always failed to deliver effective and powerful

Magic. Due to his sloppy character and experiments, he always used to get bullied by other magicians.

Anika belongs to a small farmer family. She is considered one of the best students in school for her skills in Archery. Her family always strived her to become the best farmer who grows special types of rice, which you won't get in all Prithvi. They are famous for rice which they grow, and they export it to the different parts of the world.

For years in the realm, peace thrived. Until recently, a Messenger from Sanpheran unexpectedly arrived in Kirtiyan to deliver a message from the King of Sanpheran to the Master of the School of Power and Magic. Master Manu, the Wise of the School, received the letter and showed a worried look. While looking at the masters' worry, Ishita the top disciple and also the caretaker of the school asked:

Ishita: What is it, Master? Why such a worrisome face? What's the matter? What's the letter about?

Master Manu: The letter is from the King of Sanpheran, Yagi. There have been grave matters going on in the faraway Kingdom of Bidar. For which the King needs our assistance.

Ishita: Do you think that this has to do with the treacherous evil things that the Kingdom is trying to achieve? Are they trying to resurrect the same forbidden evil which our Goddess has once laid to rest?

Master Manu: I fear the same as it.

Ishita: What should be done, Master? Give us the orders.

Master Manu: Hmmm, it's the time of grave concern. As you can see, I won't be able to go to the Kingdom due to my current condition. I won't be of any help, and there must be someone in the town to look after. I want you to gather all the disciples of the school and make an announcement in the town about the difficult times which we may have to face in the future and tell them to prepare themselves.

Ishita: As you say, Master.

Ishita then left the office of the Master and ordered

the servants to do what the Master had said.

Soon the announcement was sent to the people. People became worried and started preparing for the worst to come. There was a commotion all of sudden due to the announcement. Everyone was scared. Some went to their homes, and some went to the temple to pray to the Goddess.

With all this commotion going on, Nirdev was not having the slightest idea of what was going on. When he heard of the announcement, he approached the town hall to get a better understanding of the situation.

Nirdev: What is going on all of a sudden? He thought.

As he was approaching the town hall, he ran into Anika, who was delivering goods to one of the customers.

Nridev: Hey, Anika? Do you know what happened today? There was one announcement made by the school? Is it that dangerous that people started panicking? He asked worriedly.

Anika: Who knows? I just delivered the goods to one customer, and when I came here, everyone was either going to their homes or the temple. No one cared to reply to what I asked. Anyway, where are you going?

Nridev: I am going to the town hall. The announcement is posted there on the announcement wall. Do you want to come too?

Anika: Well, I am curious, so why not?

They both went to the town hall together to find out what is going on in the town.

In the town hall:

Nirdev: Reading the announcement: We have received a warning from the Capital of the Kingdom to prepare ourselves for the worst, which may come in the future as the Kingdom of Bidar has started to act suspiciously. Also, please, be on guard when traveling outside of the town as the numbers of monsters and wild animals have increased rapidly. Also, we need people to volunteer for the delivery of a message to the King of Sanpheran and to investigate the destruction of the Kingdom of Abhandaka. Contact

Ishita for more details.

P.S. Do not panic.

Nirdev: Hmmm..The Kingdom of Bidar, that Kingdom is very far south of the planet. Why should we be so worried about it?

Anika: If the School thinks that it is a matter of concern, then it is a matter of concern.

Nirdev: Well, the destruction of Abhandaka is a matter of concern, though. But I think what can we as a small town will be able to do in this case?

Anika: Well, then I think you should go volunteer for the delivery and ask them yourself.

Nirdev: Well, a good idea. In that way, I may get a good chance of getting myself enrolled in the Royal Army. The Army of Sanpheran is really good and pays well.

Anika: Good for you. Hope to see you in the army. (Going out of the town hall)

Nirdev: Hey, where are you going?

Anika: I have things to do. I will catch up with you later. Bye-bye.

Nirdev stands there alone, thinking of what to do next.

Flashback Scenario:

Nridev, Nitya, and Anika are playing in the park.

Nitya: Hey, do you know the story of the Legend of Raum, who wielded the holy sword of the Goddess to save the world? My Father was telling a story yesterday about it.

Nridev: Legend of Raum?

Anika: You don't know, Nridev? It's a pretty famous legend. All the towns' people know about it.

Nitya: It is about the Knight named Raum, who was chosen by the Goddess to wield her holy sword to destroy the evil, which once tried to destroy the world.

Nridev: Oh. That is so cool! Where can we find the sword of the Goddess?

Anika: It's just a legend, you dummy! (Hitting

Nridev on his head)

Nridev: Ouch! It hurts! How can you tell it's just a legend? It can be a true story. When I grow up, I would like to be like Raum. A Legendary Knight who defeats all the evil from this world. Haha!! (Giving a heroic smile)

Anika: Yeah, right, good luck with that. (Giving a disappointed look)

Nitya: Hey enough with this chit chat. Let's play hide and seek.

Nridev and Anika: Yeah!!

Present Scenario:

Nridev on the way to the school.

Nridev: Sighs. Hmm, how is the old man catching up? Ishita is a good disciple. No wonder she made it to the caretaker of the school.

Nridev enters the school. There were many disciples, and other adventurers gathered in the school hall. There was a notice put up on the notice board explaining the situation and criteria of participating in the other missions.

Later Ishita came forward and started addressing:

Ishita: Attention, please! As you know, we have received a letter from the King of Sanpheran himself for his concerns regarding the evil activities going on in the Kingdom of Bidar and the increase in the monstrous activities outside the town and city limits of the Kingdom. We are, therefore, requesting the best of the adventurers and disciples of the school to participate in the tournament for preparing yourself to go forward and deliver the message to the which our Master has for the King and also to investigate the destruction of Abhandaka further. We know that those who have gathered here have the best of the talents and skills who can defeat the monster on the way to the capital. But there can be only three candidates who can go in a group delivering the message to the King. The participants who clear all the tournament levels will be selected and the reward for the winners will be 2 million Rupees. Please register yourself and prepare for the tournament. The tournament will begin next week. May the blessings of Goddess Kirti be on you all!!

Nridev: That's a huge amount for just delivering a message and just to investigate. But oh well, who cares? I need that money. So, I am going to participate in it.

The next day in Anika's House:

Mother: It was quite a commotion yesterday. Do you think, Anika?

Anika: Yes.

Mother: I heard that something is going on in the Kingdom of Bidar. Something evil is going to come out of there.

Anika: You think so? It's very far from here. I don't understand why we are to worry about it.

Mother: Yes. But we cannot be too careful. We have to be prepared for anything that comes to us. Also, this is not the first time such a thing is happening.

Anika: Yea? When did it happen before?

Mother: It was a long time back. My Grandmother used to tell me stories of evil which came from a distant Kingdom and was so Powerful that it covered the whole world with its darkness.

Anika: Wow, Mom, you are scaring me now! (Says Sarcastically)

Mother: Anyway, Anika, have you heard about the Message delivery mission opened in the school yesterday. They are paying a good amount just to deliver the message to the capital. But first, you have to participate in the tournament.

Anika: Oh yeah? No, I was too busy doing things.

Mother: 2 Million Rupees.

Anika: What!!!??

Mother: Yeah, you heard it right.

Anika: Oh, my God! I can buy so many things from that much money. (Thinks in her mind)

Mother: I know you are very skilled in Archery, but your Father won't allow you to go there.

Anika: Yeah, I know.

Mother looking at Anika's sad face.

Mother: Oh well, cheer up. I will convince him somehow. You start with your practice and register yourself.

Anika: Really, Mom!! You are the best!!!

Anika hugs her mother.

Mother: I know you don't want to become a farmer. I can see in you that you are destined to become an archer. I can feel the will of the Goddess flowing in you. (She thinks)

Nitya's House

Father: It is time. (Looking at Nitya who was busy experimenting)

Nitya: Huh?

Father: You like experimenting with Magic, right? Why don't you try your luck in the tournament which is arranged by the school? They also have a good reward for the one who wins the tournament.

So, what do you say? Don't you want to become a Grand sage who will be praised for his unique Magic style?

Nitya, not too excited about the challenge.

Nitya: Nah. I am good.

Father angered with his reply.

Father: You get out this instance, you lazy fellow. Do something out there, achieve something. This stupid experimenting is not going to lead you anywhere. Face the world out there, face reality. That will teach you what real Magic is. Go and explore the world instead of doing useless experiments. Train yourself and prove your worth out there. Then only show your face to me.

The Frustrated Father kicks him out of the house.

Nitya: (Sighs) Oh, boy. This is going to be tiresome.

In the School:

Ishita: Master, why do we need this tournament?

Master Manu: As you see Ishita, this is not going to

be a simple task of delivering a message to the King. But it will be an adventure that will change the fate of the world.

With this, the three of them prepare themselves for the challenge and start to train themselves for the tournament.

Far of Kingdom in Bidar:

Unknown Evil King: How is the progress going on?

Unknown Evil Servent: Everything is going according to your plan, your Majesty.

Unknown Evil King: Very Good!

Next day in the town of Kirtiyan.

Everything is going as usual in the town. Our heroes are training themselves.

Nridev is trying his new attack out on a wooden log.

Nridev: Super Sonic Blade!! Heyaah!

The attack destroys the log. But also dents his sword.

Nridev: Oh, man! Now I have to go to the Bladesmith

to get the sword fixed. He is going to charge a lot for it. (Becomes sadder and looks again at the sword and say's) maybe I have to buy a new sword. Today is not my day. (Weeps silently)

On the other side of the town:

Anika goes to her Master's house for training.

Anika: Greetings Master! How have you been?

Master Anima: Well, hello there, Anika! I am doing well. What makes you come here?

Anika: As you may have heard about the tournament which is going to take place in the school. I am participating in it.

Master Anima: Well, well, well! How brave of you! Well, how did you convince your Father for that?

Anika: My mother is taking care of that.

Master Anima: Oh! Ritika! She has always supported you, good here that. So, what makes you come here?

Anika: Well, Master. I want to complete my training, which I was not able to complete because of my

Father. I want you to train me.

Master Anima: And why should I do that?

Anika: I know, Master. I was weak before. I was not able to compete with others. But now the times have changed. I have trained myself, but I need your guidance. I want to be perfect in what I do. An Archer on whom the people can rely on, trust on, depend on and count on. This monstrous world is cruel; not everyone can defend themselves against a monster. I want to help them. The tournament is just a start for what I want to achieve.

Master Anima: Hmm, I see. I can feel the will of Goddess Kirti in her (thinks the Master)

Anika: So, Master? Will you train me?

Master Anima: Yes, of course. But you know the training this time won't be that easy like before or whatever we do at school.

Anika: I am ready for anything.

Master Anima: Well then, Anika. Prepare yourself. Your training begins today.

Elsewhere in the School of Magic:

Nitya to Librarian: Where do I find the book of 'Godly magic spells' by Pancika?

Librarian: Well, that is the rarest book to have it in any library. As the legend says, the book contains heavenly Magic and only can be read in a certain language. Maybe you should try your luck to find the book in the Kingdom's capital of Sanpheran. There is a big library there. But I guess the book is so rare it's like a legend. You will find some clues as to where the book will be found.

Nitya: Too bad! I wanted to practice and learn new Magic for the tournament. (Makes a sad face)

Librarian: Oh, the tournament! Well, we have one book which might help you with the tournament. The book is in the 2nd aisle on the 3rd row of the shelf.

Nitya: Oh, okay. Thanks for the advice.

Nitya goes to the spot and finds the book. The Book of Pisakas. (His facial expression turns unwanting)

Nitya: Well, it's a lower-level Magic spells book. But

something is better than nothing.

Nitya then gets out of the Library and heads his way to the training arena, where he has to practice out his Magic spells.

Nridev goes to the Bladesmith

Nridev: Hey, Kratuvid! How are you doing?

Kratuvid is a blind bladesmith. But his swords and other weapons are best in the town.

Kratuvid: Is that Nridev? Of course, it is. I can't forget the voice of my favorite disciple cum customer.

Nridev: Oh, you still think I am your disciple? I just learned one trick from you, that's all.

Kratuvid: Well, one trick or thousand. What learned is learned. (Kratuvid laughs)

Nridev: Never mind. I came here for my sword got wrecked.

Kratuvid: Oh, is that so? Let me see it.

Nridev: But you can't see.

Kratuvid: Well, of course, I can't say let me feel it. But oh well, the wreckage is too much. It will take some time for it to get repaired and will also cost you more.

Nridev: What? No way! I have a tournament to participate in.

Kratuvid: Oh, the tournament. Well, in that case, let me show you a new sword which I made. I can lend it to you for some time.

Nridev: Will you? That would be great. Let me see it.

Kratuvid: Hold on a moment. The sword is not just a normal sword; the sword's called Soul blade. I wanted it to test the sword. So, I think you can have it and test it for me and give me the feedback. But I should warn you. The sword feeds on souls.

Nridev: Really? (Asks him in fear)

Kratuvid: Naaah, I just made up the last part. (Laughs loudly)

Kratuvid hands over the beautifully made sword to Nridev.

Nridev: Hey old man. This is a unique sword you have made. I am impressed.

Kratuvid: Well, there are many more powerful swords, which are made by Bladesmith's all around the world. You should explore when you get the opportunity. These swords are nothing compare to the Holy sword of the Goddess Kirti.

Nridev: You believe in that legend?

Kratuvid: Legend? It is true. Well, some people think about it as a legend. But. Let me tell you something; listen carefully.

Nridev listens to him carefully.

Kratuvid: The only way to find the blade of the Goddess is to have faith in yourself and the Goddess. Then only the Goddess will show you the way to where her sword is. If you want to become the chosen one, you should believe in yourself. And always keep learning. Remember, when the student is ready, the teacher will appear.

Nridev is somewhat baffled with the words from

the Bladesmith.

Nridev: I will surely try to remember it.

With this, Nridev takes the sword, thanks Kratuvid and goes on his way home. As the training continues and our heroes try their best for the tournament.

Next-Day of the training.

Nridev: Well, let's try out the new sword, Soul blade.

As the sword was a little heavy, the grip was very nice. Nridev then tries to train. He gives a slash on the log. The log gets destroyed easily.

Nridev: Wow. This is a good sword. My chances at the tournament are looking bright. (Laughs happily)

Far from the area in the woods, a dark figure was watching Nridev's training. It was a creature whose evil intent is to collect information and report it back to Bidar. These creatures were sent by the Kingdom to prepare their strategy against the incoming attack, which may happen in the future upon them. Nridev didn't notice the creature at all and continued his training.

Nridev: I should go and give feedback to Kratuvid about the sword after the training.

Nridev continues his training elsewhere in the town. Nitya was sleeping in his house.

Nitya's Father: Well, well, well! Look who's sleeping. He kicked him from his bed, shouting, get up your lousy head! It's already Noon!!

Nitya wakes up and gives a defence stance.

Nitya: Who's there? Oh. I was having a dream dad. A very good dream.

Nitya's Father: Oh yeah? What were you dreaming?

Nitya: It was a dream where I became the Great sage of Prithvi, and I was on a quest to save the princess of a certain kingdom, and all of a sudden, a group of monsters attacked me and while a was fighting them someone from the back kicked me.

Father, in regret, slaps his hands on his forehead.

Father: I don't know what will happen to you. You just dream of becoming a Great sage. But to make your dreams come true, you have to work for it. You won't be achieving it sleep like that.

Father takes a deep sigh and continues.

Father: Well, did you participate in the tournament? Did you do something for it?

Nitya: Oh, yes. I did.

Father: Okay. We will talk about it by the dining table. Get ready and come down for lunch.

Nitya: Lunch? What about breakfast?

Father gives a punch on his head.

Father: It's already afternoon! Now get ready and come down.

Nitya: Ow! Okay, okay.

Nitya readies himself and gets to the dining table for lunch.

Father: So, what are the preparations you have made so far?

Nitya: Well, I got a book of spells from the Library.

Father: And?

Nitya: Read it a bit.

Father: And?

Nitya: And nothing, came back home.

Father got angry with his answers and punched his head again.

Nitya: Ow, that hurts!

Father: Good. It should hurt. Anyway, here take this, it will help you ahead with your tournament and journey.

Father handed over him a talisman.

Nitya: Wow! It's so beautiful.

Father: Well, Yes. It is our ancestral talisman of good hope. It will always help you in difficult times.

Nitya: Father?

Nitya asked with a frowning voice.

Father: Yes?

Nitya: Why didn't you give me this earlier? I needed

something like this when I was on the verge of inventing something and failed. It would have helped me a lot then.

Father: Just shut it! I knew how worthless your experiments were. So now, take care of the talisman as the journey which you will be going will be treacherous, and difficulties will always be in your way. I pray to the Goddess for your wellbeing and safe return.

Nitya: Umm, Father, I still have a tournament to win?

Father: I know it (Punches him again on the head). I am sure that you will win. As a father, I will always hope best for you.

Nitya: Yea, right.

Father: Now, hurry up and train yourself.

Nitya: Yes, Master!

Nitya wears the talisman and leaves for training.

Anika's House.

Mother: Good Morning, Anika! Have you slept well?

Anika: Good Morning, Mom! Yes.

Mother: Good! So how is your training going on?

Anika: Very Good! Master Anima is training me well.

Mother: Oh, that's good to know. How is she doing? Been a long time, I haven't visited her.

Anika: She is doing well. She is a great master of Archery.

Mother: We have quite a talent in our town.

Anika: Yes. Okay, Mom, I better leave for my training. She doesn't like people coming late for the training, and apart from that, I am getting special training from her.

Mother: Is that so? Okay then, here is your lunch bag.

Anika: Thanks, Mom. See you later.

Anika runs out of the house and reaches Anima's place.

Anima: You are late! (Say's angrily)

Anika: Sorry, Master, got some work to do in the

house. (Started making excuses)

Anima: Enough! I don't want to hear excuses. As you know, now you are my pupil. You have to obey my rules. So, now for your punishment, you have to use sharp steel-string bows and thorny arrows and practice it 100 times, hitting the Bullseye for all the hundred times. And if you miss the Bullseye, you have to try again from 1.

Anika with surprise and fear.

Anika: Yes, Master, whatever you say.

Anika then goes to the archery range and starts to practice.

Nitya goes to the School of Magic and enters the school office.

Nitya: Can I see prof. Darbhin?

Clerk: Prof. Darbhin? He retired a long time ago. You better check his house.

Nitya: May I get his address?

Clerk: Sure. Just give me a min.

Nridev: I think today is enough of the training. Better go back to Kratuvid and give him the feedback.

Nridev then packs his things up and starts to go back to the Bladesmith.

Nridev: Well, today was an exhausting day. I hope I win the tournament.

All of a sudden, lightning strikes him, and he crashes on the road.

Unknown Voice: So, you are the one which the Master was talking about?

Nridev losses his consciousness, Nitya on his ways to Prof. Darbhin House.

Nitya: Well, I hope Professor will help me out with my doubts and teach me something new.

Suddenly the same lightning strikes Nitya, and he also losses consciousness.

Anima: Well, it's enough for today. Come back tomorrow on time.

Anika: Yes, Master.

Anika makes her way home as she was on the way. She sensed a weird black-figure presence near her as the figure was about to strike her. She cleverly dodges its attack.

Unknown figure. My, my! You are quite a unique character; you are not like those two dumb ones Nridev and Nitya.

Anika: Senses the danger and positions herself in a defensive stance.

Unknown figure: Don't you worry! It won't take long.

Anika: Who are you?

By the time she does something, the figure casts a powerful spell on her, making her unconscious. Sometimes our heroes gain consciousness, but they don't remember what had happened and why they were laying in the middle of the road.

Nridev: Uh! My head hurts!

Nitya: What happened? There was a big flash of light and then…?

Anika: Ow! Who was that? I better meet Nridev and Nitya. But my head hurts. Better go home now.

Nridev checks everything is in order with him or not and confirms that everything was okay, then moves on to meet Kratuvid.

Nitya thought that he had a mild concussion and moved on to meet Prof. Darbhin.

Nridev upon reaching the Bladesmith.

Nridev: Hey, Kratuvid! I came back to give you feedback on the sword.

Kratuvid: Hello, Nridev! So how was the training?

Kratuvid notices some strange aura coming from Nridev and asks him.

Kratuvid: Nridev?

Nridev: Yes?

Kratuvid: I feel some strange aura coming from you! It is not a usual feeling

Nridev: Aura?

Kratuvid: Yes, did something happened?

Nridev: Now that you have mentioned. My head hurts a little.

Nridev then tells him about what happened.

Kratuvid: Hmm, Let me check your forehead.

Kratuvid then places his hand on his forehead and feels a strange marking, and his hand was immediately thrown back from Nridev.

Nridev was in pain again and was a little shocked to see what happened there.

Kratuvid: Well, this is strange.

Nridev: Kratuvid! Are you alright?

Nridev goes and helps Kratuvid to get up.

Kratuvid: Yes, I am alright.

Nridev: What happened? How could this happen? I have so many questions.

Kratuvid: Ah! Don't you worry! Someone has cast a spell on you. I think someone is playing with you.

Don't worry; it will fade away in a few days.

Nridev: You sure? But what I saw didn't feel like someone playing with me.

Kratuvid: Don't worry, I just slipped. Don't get this in the way of your training and tournament.

Kratuvid understood the seriousness of the spell and the situation but didn't want Nridev to get into unnecessary trouble, so brushes off the worries and convinces Nridev as it was just a weak spell.

Nridev: If you say so. But I think you should take some rest. I, too, will get going home as today is not just my day, I think.

Kratuvid: Well, Nridev, you are right. Let's hear about the feedback of the sword tomorrow. Go back home, cautiously.

Nridev: Don't worry. I will come back tomorrow after training.

Nridev then goes back home.

Kratuvid starts to think of the evil which may come

and was worried.

Kratuvid: Well, we better get prepared and discuss this matter with Pratibahu.

Nitya reaches his destination, Prof Darbhin's House. His house was a small hut-like bungalow in front of the house there is a small lawn on the right and a flower garden on the left and on the backside faces a small pond Nitya knocks on the door of the Professor.

Nitya: Hello, Prof Darbhin! It is me, Nitya, your old student. Hello?

Nitya knocks twice, but no one answers.

Nitya: I think he must be asleep.

Nitya decides to go backside of the house. Upon reaching the backside, he saw that the Professor was sleeping on his swinging chair calmly.

Nitya: Umm, Professor? It is me, Nitya.

Darbhin: Starts talking in his sleep. "Well, now mix this potion and see what reaction it makes?"

Nitya: Oh! He is dreaming. Slaps his hand on his

forehead in agony.

Darbhin: Continues to talk in his sleep. "Yes, the chemical reaction which happens with mixing the potion is called..."

Nitya then screams in his ears to wake him up.

Nitya: PROFESSOR!!!

Darbhin wakes up surprisingly.

Darbhin: Oh, my wand! What in the world? The potion mixture exploded. Huh? Oh! It was a dream. Whew!

Nitya, with his cringed face, greets the Professor.

Nitya: Good Day, Professor! How have you been?

Darbhin looks at Nitya while adjusting his specs on his nose. He tries to recollect the face but was not able to recognize it.

Darbhin: Hello there. Do I know you? I am sorry to be rude, but my memory is giving up on me.

Nitya: How can you forget me, Professor! It is me, Nitya!

Darbhin thinks a little, scratch his head and answers.

Darbhin: Oh! I remember. You are the food delivery guy. Where is my pizza?

Nitya slaps his forehead again.

Nitya: This is going to be a headache trying to make him remember who I am.

Anika reached home and was thinking about the incident which happened on the way.

Anika's Mother: How was your day, honey?

Anika was in her world; thinking about the incident didn't notice what her mother asked her.

Mother worried about her behavior, puts her hand on the shoulder.

Mother: What's the matter, honey? Is everything okay?

Anika suddenly comes out of her thinking and answers.

Anika: Yes, mother, all is fine.

Mother then notices a strange mark on the side of her forehead.

Mother: What is the mark you got on the forehead? It was not there before, and why is it glowing?

Anika didn't notice the mark until her mother points it out for her. Then she looks at her mark in the mirror. Anika didn't want her mother to be bothered with what happened to her on the way back home. But seeing the situation that she cannot hide it from her, she narrated the ordeal which happened to her on the way.

Mother: Oh, my goodness! What is happening? The situation is going out of hand. We should report it to Sanrakshaksena about this.

Sanrakshasena is an organization, which is like a police force where people can register their complaints and. Sanrakshasena has specialized warriors, magicians, and archers employed.

Anika: No, mother! I will handle the situation, trust me.

Mother: I am worried about it. Please do take extra care now.

Anika: Yes, Mom!

Nitya: Professor, I was your student, who you used to adore?

Darbhin: Student? I retired a long ago. Those were the days when I used to experiment Magic and...

Nitya: Ahem...Sir, I think that's not the point.

Darbhin: Well, yes. Nitya? Is it?

Nitya: It will take some time for me; remember you. But in any case, may I know why did you miss a turn to this old man's house?

Nitya: Yes, Professor! I came to learn Magic from you. The Magic, which you told me earlier which cannot be learned in school.

Darbhin puts his hands on his chin and starts to think.

Darbhin: I said something like that? I don't remember.

Frustrated Nitya again slaps his hand on his forehead

and starts to narrate the things which he said in the past in the school.

At Sanrakshasena office.

Pratibahu: Well, the protection ring around the town has been tampered with. I also met Kratuvid today; he said that some strange creature has been attacking people in the town.

Dhumini: Yes, we have inspected the border area and found some strange strains on the trees where we have laid the protection shield for the town.

Pratibahu: I think we have to tighten up the security and tell all our officers to be on guard. As the tournament is fast approaching, we don't want any dangerous activities coming during that time. We will have people coming from surrounding villages and towns who will be participating in the tournament. Do not compromise on the security of the people.

Dhumini: Yes, sir! I will increase the night patrols and have everyone checked before coming and leaving the town.

Pratibahu: You have all my permission to do so.

Dhumini then goes and instructs all the officers and employees to stay on guard and increase patrols in the town.

Darbhin: Ah!! Now I remember! It's you Nitya. Nitya Brihatsena!

Nitya wipes his sweat on his forehead and gives a long sigh.

Nitya: Thank god! You remembered. Now shall we get down to business?

Darbhin: Wait a sec! Tell me one thing, first?

Nitya: Yes?

Darbhin: Why did you come here?

Nitya again slaps his head in agony.

Anika: Why did it happen? Who was that figure, thing, or whatever? I should inspect it tomorrow. Also, that thing said that something about Nridev and Nitya. I hope they are alright. I will check on them soon tomorrow morning.

Nridev reached home and on the dining, table starts to think about what happened earlier today.

Nridev: What is this mark? Why did he attack only me? There were no other incidents I heard of from the town. So, it happened only to me.

Nridev starts to wonder. The more he thinks about the incident, the more questions lurk his mind.

Nridev: No point wondering and thinking about the incident. I think I should take the advice which Kratuvid gave me not to worry about it.

Nridev then starts doing his house chores.

Darbhin: Oh, yes! The tournament, I have heard about that! So, you want my help with the tournament?

Nithya: Yes, Professor. I know that you can teach me a thing or two which you didn't teach us in the school.

Darbhin: Hmmm. Okay, Nitya! I will teach you. But I think it is getting dark now. We can start tomorrow.

Nitya wasted his day trying Darbhin to

remember things.

Nitya: Well, okay. But please don't forget about me tomorrow when I come here.

Darbhin: Don't you worry! I don't forget things that easily.

Nitya again slaps his forehead. Darbhin starts to write something on a piece of paper

Darbhin: Before coming here, bring this thing from the shop of Magic and potion just in case.

Nitya: What is this for?

Darbhin: It's a portion of Smara. It will bring my memory back for a short period.

Frustrated Nitya shouts at the Professor.

Nitya: You should have told me that before! We would have saved our precious time and started our training.

Darbhin: Sorry!

Nitya then leaves for his house, frustrated.

Somewhere in the Southern Kingdom of Bidar.

Unknown Character: Are all the preparations complete?

Unknown Character: Yes, My Lord!

Unknown Character: Good! Let the show begins!

Next-Day in Sanpheran Kingdoms Capital:

King, in his courtyard discussing the situation with his ministers and army generals.

King: As you know, the Kingdom of Abhandaka is destroyed as if there was no kingdom ever-present before.

Minister 1: Yes, my Lord! This is a grave matter of concern.

Minister 2: We just received a message from our neighboring Kingdom of Kanistha.

King: What is it?

Minister 2: They have offered their help for investigating and will assist against any worst situation which may arise in the future. They have sent their top officials for help.

King: Is that so!? They have always been a good friend of ours. Send them whatever assistance they need and take utmost care of the officials from Kanistha and involve our team of top Sanrakshasena officials with them.

Minister 2: As you say, My Lord!

A total of 5 officials from the Kingdom of Kanistha were the top warriors, sages, and archers who were selected to do the investigation on the destruction of the Kingdom of Abhandaka.

In Nridev's House. Nridev is sleeping and is having a dream.

Unknown Female Voice: There is something you should see.

Nridev: Huh? What is this? What is going on?

Unknown Voice: Don't be afraid.

Nridev sees in the distant a blur figure carrying a sword. The sword was glowing so much that he was not able to see who was holding it. The figure was coming close to him.

Nridev: Ahhh! My eyes! - He screams

Nridev then falls off from his bed and wakes up.

Nridev: That dream again!

Nridev then gets up questioning himself why does he gets such dreams nowadays and get ready for the day.

Anika: Well, Mom, I am off. See you later in the evening.

Mother: Take care, honey! And if anything happens, don't take the risk of fighting it alone.

Anika: Yes, Mom! Bye-Bye!

Anika makes her way to the house of Nridev before going to her training. She, fortunately, meets Nitya on the way.

Anika: Nitya!! Where are you up to this early morning. According to my information, you are not an early birth, to begin with.

Nitya: Huh? Well, yeah, you can say that again.

Anyway, I am participating in the tournament, so I am going for my training sessions with Prof. Darbhin. Where are you off to?

Anika: I am going to Nridev's house, and you are coming with me.

Anika grabs Nitya's hand and drags him along with her to Nridev's house.

Nitya: Hey!! Wait a minute!

In a flash, they reach Nridev's house. Nridev was locking his door and was about to leave.

Anika: Nridev, wait a minute, we need to talk!

Nridev: Anika?

Then they all sat on the bench nearby in the garden.

Anika: Did anything happened yesterday with you guys?

Nridev and Nitya look at each other and reply together.

Nridev and Nitya: YES!!

Nitya: But I thought that it was just a concussion, and I thought it happened only to me. Did you also get the same concussion?

Anika gives a beating on this head.

Anika: NO, you dummy! It was not a concussion.

Nridev: Yes, I was unconscious for a little while. But I thought it happened to me only.

Anika then shows her mark on the forehead.

Anika: Look, did you get a mark on the forehead too?

Nridev was surprised to see the mark and showed her his mark. The mark was different than hers but was having a small glow.

Anika: Nitya? Did you get the mark too?

Nitya kept silent for a little while and then proceeded to show his mark.

Anika: So, the figure of the beast or whatever who attacked me also attacked you guys too.

Nridev: There are so many questions I wanted to be answered. The main question is, why did it attack us only?

Anika: As of now, we don't know. This mark is also given to us by the beast. For now, the mark is not bothering us, but we have to be extra careful as anything may happen ahead.

Nitya: Yes, you are right! I will research these markings and will find some solutions to get rid of it.

Nridev: Hmmm, I am very concerned about this.

Anika: Don't worry! We have much bigger problems to face now. Anyway, how is your training going on?

Anika tries to normalize the situation.

Nridev: Oh! The training is going on well. How are you guys doing? I heard the tournament is going to be big and people from nearby towns and villages are participating in it.

Anika: Yes! We will be competing with the most talented warriors from other towns.

Nitya: So? It's better to go for the training rather than wasting our time here now that our main talk has been finished?

Anika: Oh, yes!! I better go, or else I would be get punished unnecessarily.

Anika runs off to her Master's house.

Nitya: Okay, Nridev. I will be seeing you later then.

Nridev: Yes, see you later!

They both part their ways to go to complete their training for the day.

Nridev: let's meet Kratuvid before I start the training- He thinks.

Kratuvid was, as usual, forging his sword when Nridev walks in his store.

Nridev: Hello, Kratuvid!

Kratuvid: Hello, Nridev, did you rest well?

Nridev: Yeah, somewhat. – Makes a pity face.

Kratuvid: Bad dream, maybe?

Nridev: How did you know?

Kratuvid: I sometimes see by my ears. Well, I guessed

by the tone of your reply. It was pretty obvious.

Nridev: Hmm, it is this dream which I often get nowadays. There is a lady with a glowing sword in her hand, and she approaches me, and the glow is bright. I wake up. I can't understand why this dream is coming to me now. I now don't know if it is even a dream or a nightmare.

Kratuvid: Hmm, can you explain to me the structure of the sword? Were you able to get a glance at the sword?

Nridev: Yeah, somewhat. The sword emits a bright light as bright as the Sun. It looks like a double-edged sword with a face engraved on the handle of the sword.

Kratuvid listens to him carefully and understands the whole dream and comes to a conclusion what the dream may have some connection with the sword of the Goddess, but he does not say anything to Nridev about it.

Kratuvid: Well, this is a weird dream you are having. I think you should not worry about it that much.

Nridev: Oh my god! You said it.

Kratuvid: Huh?

Nridev: Whenever you say not to worry, I get into trouble. – Nridev becomes sad.

Kratuvid: Hahaha! Don't worry. The Goddess is there always watching you. Anyway, you are going to train for the tournament today, right?

Nrivdev: Yes, today is the last day before the tournament.

Kratuvid: Very well kid, I will teach you a new technique which will be helpful for you for the tournament and in your future journey.

Nridev gets excited and say:

Nridev: Really?

Kratuvid: Lets prepare.

Anima: So, I think today is the last day before the tournament. I have taught you things that are needed for the tournament.

Anika: Yes, Master!

Anima then notices her glowing mark and asks.

Anima: What is that mark on your forehead? It was not there yesterday; did you overdo the training?

Anika then explains what happened to her and her friends about yesterday.

Anima: Oh, I see! So, the threat is bigger than I expected. – Anima thinks.

Anima: okay, Anika, I have got one last skill, which I need to teach you. Prepare yourself.

Anika: Yes, Master!

Nitya reaches Prof Darbhin's house. Knocks at his door and getting no response, he goes at the backside of Prof's house. Professor was having his morning cup of tea.

Nitya: Morning, Professor! Why didn't you install a decent doorbell?

Darbhin notices Nitya but did not recognize him.

Darbhin: Hello there, lad! May I know who you are?

Nitya already knew that this would happen.

So, he says.

Nitya: Well, I came from the Potion Shop and got you your delivery. The potion of Smara.

Nitya then opens the bottle of the potion of Smara and proceeds to add it in his tea.

Nitya: Please, drink it and let me know how it tastes?

Darbhin didn't remember that he had ordered such a thing but anyway proceeds to drink the tea with closed eyes. After drinking the tea, he opens his eyes with a bright shine coming from them. He gets his memory back and recognizes Nitya standing in front of him.

Darbhin: Oh, Nitya! It's you! When did you come?

Nitya: Just been a while. So, now let's not waste time and get on with the training.

Darbhin: Oh, yes, the training! Let's get started. Before we get started, you have to pass three tests which I have for you. If you are ready, then show me what you got.

Nitya: With pleasure.

The test was to check the abilities of Nitya in which the Darbhin was checking his Accuracy, Strength to execute the Magic, and ability to solve the problems put forward to him.

Nitya then demonstrates his skills of Magic to Darbhin and somehow clears all the tests which Prof had put for him and is quite impressed with his display of actions.

Darbhin: Well, Nitya! I have seen your skills and magic potential. Quite frankly, I must say that you are skilled. But you have to work on the accuracy part as you were missing the targets, actually all of them. I may for now overlook that, but you should continue to practice on that particular thing.

Nitya: I understand.

Darbhin: You have all magical skills and techniques which we have taught in the school, and you even have invented some new combination of Magic, but they are not stable.

Darbhin thinks and continues.

Darbhin: I will teach you this one magical skill that we have not taught anyone up till now in school or anywhere.

Nitya: Oh, yes, I was waiting for this moment!

All of a sudden, the stomach of Darbhin starts to growl.

Darbhin: Before we proceed. We have to do one of the most important activities.

Curious and excited, Nitya.

Nitya: What?

Darbhin: Let's have lunch before we start!

Nitya gets angry and shouts.

Nitya: You crazy old man! You got me all excited for nothing.

Then all of a sudden, Nitya's stomach also starts to growl.

Nitya blushes and says.

Nitya: Well, it's okay; we can have a bite.

Darbhin: That's my boy!

They proceed to have a quick lunch in the Professor's house. At the dining table, Darbhin notices Nitya's glowing mark on his forehead and asks.

Darbhin: That mark on your forehead?

Nitya: Oh, yeah! I was going to ask you about it.

Darbhin: Let me tell you something about the scenario of Magic here in Kirtiyan. The research potential in Magic and potion is more, yet it is very limited. We have very limited resources to get our ideas into reality or to develop unique or powerful Magic. Whatever resources we have in school or the library are not enough. You may need to travel around the world to learn Magic. Due to restricted access to other kingdoms, we up till now were not able to gain enough knowledge of their magic expertise, but we do have some knowledge of it. I may not be able to decipher the code of that mark on the forehead, but I can tell that is a curse mark that you have got.

Nitya gets a little scared and asks.

Nitya: What do you mean by curse mark? What sort of a curse? Am I going to die?

Darbhin: Well, there are many curse marks cast by the user, and only the user who cast it can give you the answers to your questions. For now, I don't think that mark looks harmful, yet you have to watch every step you take.

Nitya: Do you know any idea how to get rid of this mark?

Darbhin: Well, I am afraid I won't be able to help you out on this, but you can get rid of it.

Nitya: How?

Darbhin: First is only the caster of the curse mark can remove the mark and second only if the caster dies, then only the mark or whatever curse he has put on you will disappear.

Nitya: These are making my problems a little worse, but thanks for the information.

Nitya gets some hopes and decided to find the caster after the tournament is over.

Darbhin: Well, then, before I start the training, let's start with the overall understanding of Magic in the world of Prithvi.

Darbhin then takes the world globe and starts to explain. The globe itself magically turns only by the feather touch of the processor.

Darbhin: Okay, let's see. This is our Kingdom. The Kingdom of Sanpheran. We specialize in Elemental Magic. Do you know what Elemental Magic is, right?

Nitya: Yes, as a student of magic school, we are told about the basics of our magic forte. It is that we use elements of nature, i.e., Air, Water, Earth, and Fire.

Darbhin: Good! As expected from my knowledgeable pupil. But there is more than this.

Nitya: Huh?

Darbhin: Yes! The elements, which you mentioned are the main group of our element magic. There are various sub-groups present out there. For example, frost, which is a subgroup of water.

Nitya: Oh, I see!

Darbhin: There are various regions in the world where the magic distribution is more or less. Like the Kingdom of Sampriya is located in the hot deserts of Varcas. So, it is obvious that they have expertise in Fire magic. The types of fire magic spells they will be having will be more powerful than any other kingdom in this world. Whereas we as elemental magic users use combinations of natural elements that can surpass all other magics. Still, our lack of research in the Magic we have not been able to surpass other types of Magic.

Nitya: Yes. We have been using only basic elemental Magic up till now.

Darbhin: Hmmm, we have a history for it. Elemental Magic can be disastrous if not able to cast it properly. The Magic used in the era of Devavant was different, and the Magic used now is different.

Nitya: What sort of Magic was used in the era of Devavant?

Darbhin: Devavant was a legendary sage. He was a master of all magic spells. He was the chosen sage to fight against the evil by the Goddess. So, you can guess how powerful his Magic may have been.

Nitya started to imagine the Magic which Devavant may have used against the evil, which once tried to destroy the world.

Darbhin: Well, Nitya, I hope you understood the magical world of Prithvi?

Nitya: Yes, Professor!

Darbhin: The combinations of the magic spells can be used to the betterment of the world and or otherwise. What you do and what you achieve will decide the fate of yourself and the world.

Nitya: Yes, my goal is to be the best magician in the world, and I will do it for the betterment of the world.

Darbhin: Very well, let's get started with the training.

Nitya: Finally!

Nridev, under the guidance of Kratuvid, starts

his training.

Kratuvid and Nridev are in the practice arena.

Kratuvid: The sword fighting style which is taught in the school is the very basic one, and the main motive of the school is to train their disciples on how to defend themselves, and basic some basic combat training is taught, which is for the starters.

Nridev: Yes, I am already known with all the techniques which the school has taught.

Kratuvid: So, we are good with basics. Well, let's start with some background history before I teach you the technique. Our town was once famous for its long-lost fighting style of Ranavanya. The fierce sword-fighting technique was used by Ranavanya who battled against the evil long ago. The fighting styles which Ranavanya used were written down by the scholars and eye witness that time in the form of scrolls. When the great war broke out, the scrolls mysteriously disappeared. Some of the technique was then carry forwarded by the disciples of Ranavanya after that. But the true form of the techniques is still not known to humanity. The technique which I am going to teach you is one of the styles of Ranavanya, which you can use it in your future journey.

Kratuvid then takes his sword out of his sheath and swings it one time in a circular motion. Kratuvid, for the training, has already placed a small marble on a wooden log to demonstrate the technique. Kratuvid was around 3-4 feet away from the marble.

Kratuvid: Now watch carefully.

Kratuvid then swings his sword towards the marble in the straight forward path; his movement was also so fast that he moved to the other direction of the log, hitting the marble in a matter of seconds. The strength and speed of the swing were so severe that marble was destroyed into dust, and the dust was flying all over the place. Nitya was so amazed that he was not able to understand and was not able to see what happened there. He just saw the marble turned into dust, and Kratuvid was at the other side of the log.

Nridev: Wow! How did you do that!?

Kratuvid: You need to focus on the target. Focus on the part where you want to hit. Then gather all your strength and release the technique. Here, now you try.

Nridev: Okay!

Nridev then tries to do as Kratuvid instructed, but after several tries, he was not able to destroy the marble into dust. The marble was getting cracked or otherwise thrown away from the log. Tries after tries, Nridev gets exhausted.

Kratuvid: Hey, Nridev! Let's take a short break and have something to eat.

Nitya: Oh, yes! All this training made me hungry.

Both of them went into the inn to have lunch.

Anima and Anika get ready for their training in the ranch.

Anima: okay, Anika, we are in the last part of the training now, and you have shown immense improvement in your Archery. But now what I am going to teach you is the combination of all the training techniques we have done so far.

Anima takes a deep breath and continues.

Anima: There are many archery styles in the world, but we are going to learn, and we are known with the style of Adrishyanti. Of course, the style which Adrishyanti used is not known much now, but we know some of it.

Anima winks and tells her.

Anima: The style which I am going to teach you is the Elemental Arrow of Adrishyanti.

Anika: Elemental Arrow?

Anima: Yes! The arrow has all the major elements such as Fire, Air, Water, and Earth. Here let me show you.

Anima then takes her bow and arrow and aims to the four leaves which were tied for the training. As the arrow is released from the bow, the arrow multiplies in two-four arrows of fire, air, and water and strikes all the leaves burning one leaf, wets and cuts other leaf cuts the leaf into pieces, and other earth elemental arrow was not able to damage much to the leaf.

Anima: See? It is how it is executed. Saw the leaves? Out of the four, only three were destroyed as the leaf was weak against those elements, but the earth was not able to damage it as leaves have some resistance against the earth.

Anika: Oh, I see!

Anima: There are many techniques in the world. You have to explore them to learn them. The most powerful is the Archery styles of Adrishyanti.

After a pause, Anima continues.

Anima: Now, you give a try.

Anika: Yes, Master!

Anika then starts to practice the Elemental arrow of Adrishyanti.

By the end of the day:

Nridev huffing and lying on the down due to exhaustion.

Kratuvid: Well, well, well! So how did it go?

Kratuvid checked the log to find the marble was still on the log. He took the marble and said:

Kratuvid: If you still can't master this basic technique, then how will you survive the tournament.

Nridev then snatches the marble from the hands of Kratuvid and perform the style of Ranavanya "The Rapid Flash style." The marble was destroyed into dust particles in front of Kratuvid. He performed the technique while the marble was still in the air, and all the dust flew around Kratuvid. Feeling that he has achieved what was designated to Nridev, Kratuvid smiled a little and was feeling proud. He thought that the one who can go and achieve the Legacy of Ranavanya is going to be Nridev.

Kratuvid: I thought you were not going to pull it off! The technique took me months to master. But I give it to you, you have quite a talent and have amused me.

Nridev huffing and smiling with tears of joy while listening to Kratuvid and faints.

Nitya and Darbhin continue their training.:

Darbhin places an unusual opal shaped material that seemed like titanium.

Darbhin: Here, this is an Obsidian stone. One of the most powerful metals from which people make armors and swords. It is so strong that it cannot be destroyed that easily.

Now, I want you to destroy the stone. Use whatever Magic you know and destroy it. It will be good even I see a crack on the stone.

Nitya: That's it? This should be easy.

Darbhin: We will see. Go ahead, give your best shot.

Nitya then thinks.

Nitya: Okay! This should be no problem. But by the description of the stone, I think it is not going to be an easy task.

Nitya then goes ahead and tries to use all his magic capabilities to destroy the stone. By the end of the day, Nitya was not able to make a crack on the stone. Using all the knowledge of the Magic he started to realize that he is failing, but Darbhin comes and tells him.

Darbhin: okay, Nitya, I don't see a crack on the stone yet.

Nitya: Does this thing even destructible? – Ask frustratedly.

Darbhin: Hahaha!! If it wasn't, then I would not have given it to you to destroy it in the first place.

Nitya becomes sad and gives a hopeless look.

Darbhin: All things come and go in this world; there is nothing that cannot be destroyed. You just got to know the solution to the problem and see where you can find the weak spot stone.

Nitya: Weak spot of the stone? How is that possible? How will a stone have a weak spot?

Darbhin: Tell me, what sort of Magic you used on the stone to destroy it?

Nitya: I used all sorts of fire, water, earth, and air.

Darbhin: I see. So, whatever you are doing is using these elements of Magic one by one to destroy the stone, right?

Nitya: Yes?

Darbhin: Have you tried considering using the elements all at once?

Nitya: All at once? How to do that?

Darbhin then put forward its hands, murmur something, and shine of rays comes from his hands and cracks the stone in half. Nitya was amazed to see such sort of Magic.

Darbhin: If you can't get a solution with one formula, apply multiple formulas to get an answer.

Darbhin then continues him to teach the Rays of WAFE magic.

Nitya was able to make a crack on the stone. And so, our heroes trained and got ready for the tournament.

Elsewhere in the Kingdom of Sanphenran. The special envoy who came from the Kingdom of Kanistha for the aid and helping Kingdom to investigate the ongoing crises.

Nabhi, who is the captain of the envoy.

Nabhi: Well, we succeeded in gaining the trust of the court's men without any problems.

Kripi: Yes, Master. Now we have to look for a good time to start with our plans.

Nabhi: Yes, before that, send a report to the Master in the Kingdom of Bidar about our current position and situation.

Kripi: As you say, Master.

Nabhi: Also, have they participated in the tournament taking place in Kirtiyan?

Kripi: Yes, Master. Everything is going according to the plan.

Nabhi: Good!

Our heroes are confidently training themselves for the new tournament day.

Nridev, Nitya, and Anika goes to there mentors and take their blessing for the success in the tournament and proceeds to the arena. They all meet at a junction before the arena. Anika notices Nridev walking in ahead of her and shouts his name running towards him.

Anika: Nridev! Wait for me.

Nridev looks back and waits for her.

Nridev: So, prepared?

Anika: You bet.

Nridev notices her new bow and arrow kit, which was shining like a newly purchased set.

Nridev: Nice set of bow and arrows you purchased for the tournament.

Anika: No, it is a gift from my Master.

Anika notices his sword and asks.

Anika: You too have something new?

Nridev: Well, yes. But it is not a gift, though. It's like I have borrowed it from Kratuvid.

Anika: Is that so? Anyway, where is Nitya?

Nridev: He must be waiting at the entrance

of the arena.

Nridev and Anika went to the entrance of the arena.

Nitya sees them from far and waves at them, shouting their names.

Nitya: Nridev, Anika over here!!

Nridev: So, prepared?

Nitya: Never been so nervous! What about you, guys?

They both noticed that Nitya also got something new, which they haven't seen before.

Anika: Oh! What kind of a bracelet is that? I haven't seen that before.

Nitya then flaunts the bracelet and says.

Nitya: Cool! Isn't it? It was given to me by Professor Darbhin. I will demonstrate the power of the bracelet in the tournament. Hahaha!!

Nridev: Yea, we will see.

Anika: Anyway, guys, let's go to the arena.

Nridev and Nitya: YES!!

They all went to the arena where they don't know what is going to happen; what lies ahead is going to decide the fate of the Kingdom of Sanpheran. In this way the treacherous journey of our heroes begins...